P9-DHF-971

3 4694 001356187

Library Media Center

Dover Middle School

Dover, NH 03820

Cochecho
Reader

Rosalie, My Rosalie

THE TALE
of a
DUCKLING

JACQUELYN MITCHARD

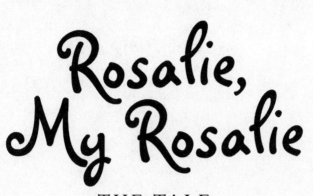

Rosalie, My Rosalie

THE TALE
of a
DUCKLING

Illustrated by

JOHN BENDALL-BRUNELLO

HARPERCOLLINS*PUBLISHERS*

Rosalie, My Rosalie: The Tale of a Duckling

Text copyright © 2005 by Jacquelyn Mitchard

Illustrations copyright © 2005 by John Bendall-Brunello

All rights reserved. No part of this book may be used or reproduced in
any manner whatsoever without written permission except in the case of brief
quotations embodied in critical articles and reviews. Printed in the United States
of America. For information address HarperCollins Children's Books, a division
of HarperCollins Publishers, 1350 Avenue of the Americas, New York, 10019.

www.harperchildrens.com

Library of Congress Cataloging-in-Publication Data

Mitchard, Jacquelyn.

Rosalie, my Rosalie : the tale of a duckling / written by Jacquelyn
Mitchard ; illustrated by John Bendall-Brunello.— 1st ed.

p.   cm.

Summary: A nine-year-old girl named Henry, who lovingly cares for her pet
duckling, Rosalie, faces a difficult decision after Rosalie grows to adulthood.

ISBN 0-06-072219-3 — ISBN 0-06-072220-7 (lib. bdg.)

1. Ducks as pets—Juvenile fiction. [1. Ducks as pets—Fiction. 2. Pets—
Fiction.] I. Bendall-Brunello, John, ill. II. Title.

PZ10.3.M635Ro 2005

[Fic]—dc22   2004019110

                                                                                      CIP

                                                                                       AC

Typography by Amy Ryan

1 2 3 4 5 6 7 8 9 10

❖

First Edition

For Alyssa and Gordon,
my heart and my hope,
and the counter lady at LaGuardia

ACKNOWLEDGMENTS

The author wishes to thank the beleaguered airline employee who first shared a part of her own childhood that led to this story. For Melanie Donovan, Kate Jackson, and Josette Kurey, a hug of thanks for faith in me. And to John Bendall-Brunello, the gifted illustrator who brought Rosalie to life, thanks for making me look good.

TABLE OF CONTENTS

Lucky Duck

Although it made her sad, Henry was a girl.

It wasn't being a *girl* that made her sad.

She liked wearing dresses to parties, putting on her mother's makeup and smiling in the mirror like a movie star, and wearing pink ballet shoes, especially while walking through big puddles. She also liked being able to climb a tree faster than any boy in her neighborhood, including boys who were older than nine.

One thing that bothered Henry was being a girl named after her father, instead of being named Sara or Vanessa or even Nancy, after her mother.

But what bothered her most was how perfectly happy her mother and father were with their nice, quiet house and their nice, (usually) quiet little girl. The way Henry saw it, too much quiet stops being so nice.

So one soft spring night, Henry asked her father the kind of question he would have to answer. She asked, "Did you *really want* a boy?"

Henry's father was resting after a day's work in the big garden he owned, so at first he didn't answer. (Answering often took him a long time, sometimes *overnight*.) Everything about Henry's father was big and slow and gentle, from his hands to his voice to the way he treated his vegetables. Gardening was her father's business. He sold fruit and vegetables to markets and restaurants.

After Henry had waited so long that she thought he might have fallen asleep, her father finally said, "Nope."

"Nope? That's all? Nope?" Henry asked. *Nope,* she was thinking. *I sat here ten minutes for 'nope'?*

"Nope," said Henry's dad, who was stretched out on the living-room floor with his massive feet sticking straight up at the ceiling like canoe paddles and his straw hat over his eyes. (He said resting like this each night helped keep his back strong, because he spent the whole day bent over the asparagus and strawberry beds. Every restaurant in town wanted to buy his asparagus and strawberries, because they were the biggest and most beautiful around. When people asked him why his strawberries and asparagus were so plump and sweet, he paused, and then, very slowly, gave them one answer: "Love." He breathed love onto those plants all year long. People said that Hank loved his garden so much, he practically kissed the strawberries and asparagus good night.)

But now he said, "Nope, I didn't want a boy."

"So how come I have a boy's name? And how come you didn't want a boy, too? Or," Henry added carefully, "perhaps a horse?"

Henry's father stroked his chin the way he sometimes petted his strawberry plants, as if they were little toddlers who needed a tickle. He tickled Henry too for a moment, and said, "No, Henry. I wanted a girl, but I wanted a girl just like me. Maybe that was kind of selfish, but that was what I dreamed about. A tall and strong girl, with hair yellow as a duck's tail feathers. And I got just what I wanted. So the minute I saw you, I said to myself, I got lucky. She's my piece of luck! But there was a problem. I always promised myself I'd name my child after my father, your grandpa. And his name is Henry. So there I was." He wiggled his toes in their gray socks, which were so big that when Henry tried them on, they still went all the way up to her knees.

Henry secretly looked down at her own feet.

She hoped she wouldn't take after her father in *every single* way.

"Well, anyhow, I was thinking," Henry whispered, crouching down right next to her father's suntanned ear, "if you did *want* a boy, we *might* have a baby. I'm almost nine now, and I wouldn't mind. In fact, it's a little boring around here. A baby, or maybe a cat?"

"Well," her father said, *very* slowly, "your mom and I have thought about that. More isn't always better. We *could* move to a farm, and have a bigger garden and a big orchard. But then, maybe, and I'm not saying for sure, but just maybe, we wouldn't be able to give that farm so much love. And that's how we feel about you. We got the best, so why bother with the rest? As for a cat, well, cats make me sneeze. They make you sneeze, too. And we can't have a horse in our neighborhood."

Henry sighed.

It wasn't that she was really lonely. She *did* have other kids to play with, if she walked up the hill and past the golf course, where most of the other houses were. There was her best friend, Livy, and the twins, Denny and Dave. She liked them, and they liked her, too, though the twins were only little kids, still in second grade, a whole year younger than Henry.

But she did not understand why her parents could be *so* slow and *so* stubborn about adding one little baby or even a very small pet. A bird? A hamster? A goat to mow the gigantic lawn?

Still, as Henry's parents pointed out, they did have a dog. But Scout, who followed Henry's father around all day, and chased the birds away from the asparagus and strawberries, wasn't much interested in playing with Henry. He was a serious dog, just like another grown-up. Scout was nice to Henry, but when she wanted him to run and jump, he preferred stretching out, with his massive paws pointed straight out in front of him, in the door of his doghouse beside the garage. Slowly. *Boringly.*

Still hopeful, Henry spoke to her

mother later that week. Henry's mom worked at the library in Henry's school. They had just finished reading about a mother duck with eight babies, and her mother was proud that Henry could read so well by herself. Being proud puts any mom in a good mood.

"You know," Henry said, "I'm almost nine now. I don't need much to take care of me. It's probably okay if you have another baby. Or get a kitten."

"Well, Henry," said Henry's mom, "we've thought about that. We had to wait a long time for you, and when you finally came, we thought, well, this is our piece of luck. A little girl with hair as yellow and soft as a baby duck's tail. And we didn't want to push our luck. So we stuck with our sweet girl."

Henry sighed.

"Aren't you happy, Henry? With Dad and Scout and me?" Mom asked.

"Yes," Henry said. "But Scout, you have to admit, is kind of a boring dog. He won't even chase a ball. He's *Dad's*."

"But we're *yours*," said Henry's mother, and kissed her on both eyelids.

"How about that kitten?" Henry asked softly, as her mother closed the door.

"Kittens make you sneeze," Henry's mom said. "And Scout *would* chase a *cat*!"

Henry sighed. Sometimes she wished her parents would disagree about something!

That night, as she often did while she was falling asleep, Henry heard her parents laughing and talking in the next room. She heard her father say, "Well, those houses up the hill *are* pretty far away. . . ."

And her mother said, "No one ever *told* us we couldn't. . . ."

She fell asleep a little sadly, thinking Scout had Dad, and Mom and Dad had each other, but all she had was her doll, a doll with the girliest name she could think of, Elizabeth Eliza Amelia, a doll her grandma had sewn with yarn hair as yellow as Henry's.

Early next morning, even though it was a Saturday, Henry heard her father's voice booming up the stairs: "Henry Marie! I need you down here right now!"

Henry jumped out of bed, pulled on her overalls, tucked Elizabeth Eliza Amelia under her pillow, and ran. The last time her father yelled out *that* loudly, he'd been about to burn the brush pile. Whatever it was, Henry didn't want to miss it.

There was Dad, standing at the bottom of the stairs in his overalls, which were just like Henry's, only seventeen sizes larger. He wasn't doing anything special. His overalls looked the same as every other day, except—Henry noticed—something was bulging out of the top of his chest pocket. Suddenly, a fuzzy little yellow head with a rosy beak popped out of Dad's pocket as well.

"A duck!" Henry cried. "Dad, you found a baby duck!"

"And not any baby duck!" Dad said. "Why, just listen to this story!"

Dad sat down, and Henry thought, *Oh boy, how long is this going to take?*

She couldn't wait to touch the baby duckling's sweet little face. It was already cheeping and struggling to get free. "I was delivering asparagus and strawberries to that fancy new restaurant in town," Henry's father said. "And I went down the back stairs."

"And then what?" Henry asked, as her dad seemed to be about to take a long pause.

"Well," he said, "down there, in the basement, among the wine boxes, was a crate of vegetables."

Sheesh, thought Henry, *oh, wow! Imagine finding a crate of vegetables!*

"But behind that crate was another

crate," said her dad. "And in that crate was the most beautiful little duckling I ever saw in my life, and do you know what?"

"What?" Henry gasped.

"That little duckling was only five hours away from being served up on a plate along with some wonderful asparagus and a reduction of strawberry sauce!"

"Oh, no!" Henry whispered, shocked. (She and her family never ate meat at all.)

"And so I said, well, that duckling's fuzzy head reminds me of something. I couldn't think what," Dad said, leaning back against the stairs. Henry was ready to jump up and down with impatience. Finally, very slowly, he said, "It reminded me of *your* hair, sticking up out of your blanket, when you were just a little baby. I checked and she was a girl, just like you! So I thought, no one is going to eat this little duckling! And so, do you know what I did?"

Henry asked, "What?"

She didn't really care, since she only wanted to pet the duckling's soft yellow down and her eager little beak, but she listened. Her dad went on, "I traded part of my load of asparagus and strawberries for this little duckling!"

"You mean for me?" Henry asked. "Is she mine, all mine?"

"She's yours," Dad said. "But you're going to have to build a pen with me, with mesh on the top so the hawks don't make a dinner of her after all, and you'll need to find a big pan for her to learn to swim. . . ."

But Henry was practically climbing up onto her dad's head with excitement and joy. Gently, ever so gently, she lifted the duckling out of her father's overalls pocket. And the duckling flapped her tiny stubbly wings once, and then rubbed her head against Henry's arm, with a touch softer than the brush of an angel's wing.

"You got lucky, ducky," said Henry, trying not to think of what *might* have happened to her brother and sister ducks.

"She's one lucky duck, and she's your piece of luck," Dad said.

"She sure is. Oh, Dad, thanks! I'm going to name her the most beautiful name I know," Henry said, stroking the little duck's rosy-brown beak. She closed her eyes and thought. She thought very hard, but very quickly. "Her name is Rosalie. Rosalie, Rosalie."

The little duck peeped, and curling up on Henry's arm, she fell asleep. Henry leaned over and whispered, "Oh Rosalie, my Rosalie. You're just a duck. But you're my piece of luck. And you mean everything to me."

That's Rosalie All Over

Henry had never learned anything in school more quickly than she learned all about ducks.

She learned what diseases they could get, and how warm and how cool they needed to be to stay healthy. She learned that they had to swim to strengthen their legs and wings, and that they could turn upside down and hold their breath. She learned that they could fly long distances if they had to, but that sometimes they preferred to walk or to swim.

She learned the special mix of grains and pieces of lettuce that would keep Rosalie growing.

And she learned about imprinting. She learned *that* all at once.

It wasn't quite summer yet, and too cold outside for a baby duck, so Rosalie's first pen was in Henry's room. Henry and her dad built a box from wire and wooden slats with a top that opened and locked with a hook. The bottom was covered with newspapers; there was a great big shallow bowl of water that Rosalie could flap and paddle in, a food tray and drinking bottle, and torn pieces of soft rag and tall grass that Henry's mother said would make Rosalie as comfortable as she had been in her own mother duck's nest. But Henry didn't want to put Rosalie in the pen. And Rosalie certainly didn't want to go into the pen, either.

The first thing Henry noticed about Rosalie was that every time Henry turned around, Rosalie was there.

She was there when Henry got a glass of milk out of the refrigerator. She was there when Henry helped her

father pull weeds. She even followed
Henry happily into the shower.

In fact, it seemed the only time
that Rosalie rested was when Henry
was out playing or doing her chores.
No matter how quietly Henry tried
to tiptoe up the stairs, by the time
she got to the door of her room,
Rosalie would be hopping up and

down, up and down, begging to be
let out of her pen. The only way
Henry knew that Rosalie rested at all
was because she was able to sneak in
one day when a thunderstorm was
going on and Rosalie couldn't hear
Henry's stocking feet on the stairs.

Henry's mother read Henry a
story that she found on the computer

that said baby ducks imprint on the first moving thing they see when they're no more than little cheeplings—even if that thing happens to be a vacuum cleaner. Usually, though, it's a mother duck. Baby ducks follow their mothers everywhere, learning how to swim, how to cross roads safely, what to eat, and what not to eat, which both teaches them and keeps them safe. "That's quacking good sense," said Henry's mom. "I wish baby people would do that!"

The story went on to say that if baby ducks don't have mothers, sometimes they imprint on other creatures, such as friendly dogs.

Henry's mother showed Henry a picture of a little duck sitting next to a big poodle, and both of them seemed to be smiling (although ducks always look as though they're smiling).

Henry's mom explained that because Rosalie had been taken from her mother at such a very young age—*And for such a wicked reason,* Henry thought—she'd imprinted on Henry.

Rosalie thought that Henry, although not a duck, was her mother.

"Why, that's the sweetest thing I ever heard of," Henry said, and she hugged Rosalie softly.

When Livy came over after school, and saw how Rosalie followed Henry everywhere she went, she was so jealous that she wanted a duck, too, although she had two Siamese cats and a whole gigantic tank full of tropical fish (which Livy considered to be about as much fun as wallpaper).

But Livy wouldn't have been so jealous if she'd spent the night in Henry's room. The trouble had started the first night Rosalie was at home. Henry had gently lowered her into her cage. After splashing in and out of her pan for a few moments, Rosalie began to jump up and down, flapping her stubby little wings as if she were having a ducky temper tantrum.

"What's the matter, Rosalie?" Henry asked, lifting Rosalie out of the pen. Well, once Henry picked her up, nothing was the matter at all. When Henry put Rosalie back, another tantrum!

It was just that Rosalie didn't want to be alone.

Henry didn't know what to do. She was pretty sure that her parents hadn't made a rule about ducks sleeping in the bed, but only because they hadn't thought of it.

So, she thought, *since they hadn't made a rule, well, why not?* And before she knew it, Rosalie had settled down into a little puffball, tucked her graceful little head under her wing, and fallen asleep on Henry's pillow.

"Oh Rosalie, my Rosalie," Henry said, touching her back and feeling her tiny heart's strong, swift beat. "You may be a duck, but you're my piece of luck, and you mean everything to me."

And Henry went to sleep, too.

In the morning, however, she learned why her parents *might* have made a rule about ducks sleeping in beds—and also why she was supposed to replace the newspapers and rags and grasses on the bottom of Rosalie's cage every day.

It took about a half hour of hard scrubbing with her fingernail brush to get the little gob of green goo off Henry's pillowcase. And even when she made her bed, after using her mother's hair dryer to get the pillowcase dry, Henry knew she had a problem.

Henry thought things over. She couldn't bear to hurt Rosalie's feelings by making her sleep in her pen.

She couldn't bear to roll in the green gook, either.

So, trying to be very easygoing about it, she asked her mother, "Do we have any baby diapers? From when I was little?"

"For Elizabeth Eliza?" asked Henry's mother, who was busy at her computer.

"Ummm, yes, they would probably fit my doll," Henry said. It wasn't quite a lie. She didn't like to lie on purpose, unless it was absolutely necessary.

"I don't think so," Henry's mother said. "But I can pick up a package of diapers at the store next time I go shopping. You don't need more than a couple, do you?"

"Uh, no," Henry said, thinking quickly. Denny and Dave had a baby sister, Derry. She was only two or three months old. They had to be able to share some diapers with Henry, too. Who would miss a couple of diapers, especially if they had seven-year-old twins and a baby?

That afternoon, while her mother was shopping, Henry carefully typed "baby ducks" into her mother's computer.

The worst was true.

Ducks simply had a habit of "going" wherever they wanted. No one could train a duck to use a litter box, like a kitten, though some people had been able to use special treats to teach their ducks to go flop outside, like dogs.

But Rosalie was still too little for that.

So, each night, thinking her parents had no idea, Henry waited until her parents had kissed her good night, while Rosalie impatiently jumped up and down, up and down in her pen. Then Henry lifted her out and fastened one of the tiny baby diapers around Rosalie's double-tiny waist.

At first, Rosalie fought more like a baby wildcat than a baby duck. But

after a while, she
seemed to figure
the diaper wasn't
going to hurt her,
and she settled down.
Henry wished she
could take a
picture of a duck
in a diaper. But she settled for drawing one, the best she could, because
she knew her parents would see the
photo if she used her mom's camera.

However, her mother and father
didn't need a picture to figure out
what was going on.

After a few weeks, when Rosalie
was losing her down and getting her

beautiful white-and-lemon-colored feathers, Henry's mom said, "Funny how many diapers Elizabeth Eliza is using, isn't it?"

Henry blushed. Together, Mom and Henry visited the vet, who gave them a little box of pellet treats the vet said no duck in her right mind could resist and a pamphlet about house-training pets.

Every time Rosalie started to flop in the house, Henry had to grab her and run outside, pulling a pellet out of her pocket. She would also take Rosalie out into the yard every morning before she left for school and again as soon as she got home and once more before they went to bed. When Rosalie flopped on the grass, Henry hugged her and said, "Oh darling duck! Rosalie, my Rosalie, you may be a duck, but you're my piece of luck! And you mean everything to me!" And Rosalie laid her growing-long neck against Henry's leg and smiled her sweet duckly smile.

As spring turned into summer, Rosalie had fewer and fewer accidents. She was so smart that soon she stood at the door, ready to go flop and get a treat.

Beware of Duck

As Rosalie grew older, she slowly got comfortable sleeping in her own nest, so long as Henry moved the pen close to her bed and spoke softly to her, stroking her head, before they fell asleep.

She also got bolder about other things.

Whenever Henry went up the hill

to play with the twins or Livy, Rosalie followed along behind, even though the hill was a pretty hard trek for a medium-sized duck, especially on hot days. Sometimes Henry had to carry Rosalie under one arm. The best fun they had was swimming in the pond behind Livy's house. The people who owned the house before Livy's family just loved fish, which was why they'd put a huge tropical fish tank in the living-room wall. They'd also built a pond for giant goldfish, but giant goldfish gave Livy's mother the creeps. So she dug the pond deeper, covered the bottom with smooth rocks, and made a little swimming pool. She filled it with water from the hose and washed it down with vinegar whenever it got a little slimy.

Unfortunately, the pool got a lot slimier when Rosalie went swimming with the girls.

Livy's mom was a very nice person, but she was a busy doctor. She didn't want to have to clean that rock pool every single day. So one day, she gently told Henry that Rosalie would be better off swimming at the little creek or ponds up on the golf course. Livy, who loved watching Rosalie turn upside down, tried sassing her mom, but all that got was Rosalie and Henry sent home and Livy sent to her room to fold laundry.

Every evening, at twilight, after the golfers were gone, Henry took Rosalie to swim in the ponds on the golf course. They were water hazards

for the golfers, but they were water parks for a duck. Rosalie was happy paddling on the eighth, tenth, and especially the seventeenth hole.

Things went okay most of the summer, until it was almost time for school to start.

That's when Rosalie, by then a fully grown duck, became a sort of hazard herself.

Up to then, Henry and her parents considered Rosalie a very useful pet. She was a far better watchduck than Scout had ever been a watchdog. Scout never took the trouble to bark, except at birds. Henry's father often said that Scout would help the burglars open the back door so long as they had a couple of liver treats on them.

But not Rosalie.

One day when Henry was drawing with sidewalk chalk, she heard a mighty *squawk!* Taking off at a run, Henry found Rosalie, her beautiful lemony-yellow wings spread wide and her long soft neck stuck straight

out, chasing the mailman up the hill.

"Rosalie!" Henry screamed. Rosalie looked back with a sweet beaky smile. She waddled over and laid her head against Henry's leg.

"Would that thing bite?" the mailman called, straightening his socks.

"I don't think so," Henry called. "She's just very protective. She's imprinted on me, you know."

"Well, she was almost imprinted by this mailbag on her head!" the mailman said, handing Henry the mail as Rosalie smiled up between them.

"See?" Henry said. "She's fine now."

"You'd better get her a chain or something," the mailman warned Henry. "That duck could really be dangerous!"

Henry thought the mailman was going a little bit overboard. But disaster struck two nights later, when she took Rosalie for her evening swim on the golf course. In the gentle light, Henry sat with her back against a tree, reading her book, while Rosalie swam and snapped happily at the bugs gliding past on the water.

All of a sudden, there was a huge squawk and an even bigger shout. Henry looked up from her book to see

a groundskeeper, who was *fortunately*
a seventh-grader Henry knew a little
from school. He was raising a rake
over Rosalie's head.

"Stop!" Henry cried. "That's my duck!"

"Your *duck* just bit **my** TOE!" the boy called back angrily, but he lowered his rake.

"Are you hurt?" Henry asked.

"No, but . . . Hey, what does this duck think? That he owns the place?" The boy seemed more scared than mad. *Big baby,* Henry thought.

"*He* is a *she*," Henry said politely. "And her name is Rosalie." Hearing her special word, Rosalie laid her sleek, wet head against Henry's leg. "She probably thought you were going to hurt me. She's imprinted on me. I raised her, her whole life."

They both looked down at the boy's toe. There *was* a little red mark. "Well, I guess I'm okay," said the boy. "But you'd better get a leash or a bell for that duck, or someone's going to make her into duck soup."

"Not that!" said Henry, her eyes filling with tears. "But I do have a problem. I wish I lived on a farm with a pond! You see, she has to swim, and I've got to take care of her, or my dad will give her to one of his farmer friends. . . ."

"You could take her to the arbor, over behind the highway. There's lots of ponds there, and lots and lots of ducks," the boy said, sitting down on his golf cart and smiling.

"I'm, uh, nine?" Henry said softly. "I know I look like I'm older, but that's only because I'm tall. My parents would never let me ride my bike across the highway, and how would I get Rosalie across?"

"It's a tough spot," said the boy. "And what's going to happen after these little water holes freeze up?"

"I don't know," Henry said sadly. "I'm *sure* my dad is going to come up with some great idea, like donating her to the petting zoo."

"Well, you'll think of something before that happens," the boy said, reaching out a little nervously to touch Rosalie's head.

"It's okay, sweetie," Henry told Rosalie, and she nuzzled the boy's hand.

"She's really a nice duck, basically," the boy said.

"She's the best," Henry said, thinking, *And she's my piece of luck, and she means everything to me.*

Rosalie on the Road

On the second day of school, while the sun was still high in the sky, Henry and her mother were driving home. Henry thought, *Well, here goes!* She took a deep breath and said, "Mom, I have an idea. Do you think you could drive me over to the arbor center a couple of times a week? After school? Or before school?

Rosalie and me?"

"Well, Henry, I could try," Henry's mother said kindly. "But they are starting the new media center, and I'm feeling a little tired these days after school. . . ."

"What about Dad?"

"Dad's got his new baby apple trees to take care of, and the asparagus and strawberries to get bedded down," her mother said.

"It's not like I'm asking you to take me to Italy!" Henry snapped. There was a map of the world on the class-room wall in fourth grade.

"Well, Henry! It's not worth sassing me! I'll try my best," said Henry's mom.

"I'm sorry," Henry told her mother quietly.

"I know," Mom replied. "And now that you've brought it up, we have been meaning to talk to you anyway." She pulled off the road near a field of sunflowers and stopped the car. "We always knew the time would come when Rosalie couldn't sleep in the house anymore. And now that time is here. The fact is, she's not a little duckling anymore. She's noisy, and . . . she smells."

"Smells?" Henry cried. "That's not fair. I clean her cage every day!"

"Well, she's far too big for that cage anyhow, and no matter how much you clean up after her, she's just making our whole house smell ducky, and right now, that smell is really bugging me," said Henry's mom. "So we're going to have to build her a bigger cage out in the garage."

"The *garage*?" Henry gasped.

"Well, Scout sleeps outside in the winter. It's not going to kill her," said Henry's mom. "All the ducks in the arbor center stay outside in the winter. Why, I used to take you to feed them when you were a tiny little girl. And Henry, remember the boy who works at the golf course? His mother called me. It was only a little bite on his toe, but she thought, I guess, that her son was going to get rabies or something. We can't have Rosalie wandering around anymore."

"But wandering around after me is her most favorite thing in the world!"

"Well, she's a little bit too much of a watchduck for that. And Henry, that's that," Mom said, starting the car. "Dad and I have talked this over—"

"Without me?" Henry gasped.

"Yes, and Dad's going to build her a wire run outside so she can walk around, and a little door in the garage wall she can walk right through back into her cage."

The thought of Rosalie down

there all alone in that dark garage
made Henry want to puke. But she
didn't have a better idea, and at
least Rosalie wasn't being sent to
the petting zoo.

The following Saturday, Henry's
mother did drive her and Rosalie to
the arbor center. Strictly speaking, the
arbor center was a botanical garden,
and it was owned by the university.
But there was a gate that everyone
knew about, and the best place to feed
corn kernels to the ducks was right
under the sign that said, PLEASE DO
NOT FEED THE WILD DUCKS. There were
always a whole bunch of little kids
down there. Of course, Henry got a

lot of attention for arriving with her very own duck.

All the little kids wanted to feed Rosalie, and she could hardly get near the water, because she politely wanted to eat all the bread crumbs and corn kernels offered her. When she finally got into the pond, all the wild ducks scurried down and swirled around her. They were little black coots and green-headed mallards. Among them, Rosalie looked as large and beautiful as a fairy-tale swan.

She seemed very excited to see other ducks.

She swam with them, climbed up on the rocks with them, and nibbled

at the algae with them. In fact, Henry
could hardly coax her out of the
water when it was time to go home.

As they drove back to their house,
Henry's mom said quietly, "She sure
seemed to enjoy that, Henry."

Henry wasn't dumb. She had

noticed the very same thing. And it made her want to cry so hard, her throat hurt. It didn't take her mother to tell her what was probably true— that Rosalie, now that she was grown up, might be happier with other ducks than with a little girl.

But Henry was *Rosalie's* little girl!

She stroked Rosalie's head and asked, "Rosalie, do you want to go live in the pond with the other ducks? I won't mind. I think you have a right to have a duck's life." But Rosalie just laid her head against Henry's hand and smiled her peaceful duckly smile.

That night, when Henry went to bed, she dreamed of Rosalie marrying a handsome green duck with a crown on his head.

It was a quiet September, but then Halloween came.

Excited to see all the children, Rosalie got out of her pen. The lock was a little loose and all it took was one lunge.

She chased one mummy, two Frankenstein's monsters, and a robot all the way up the hill, where a car filled with two witches, a princess,

and an elephant (plus their mother) nearly ran her over. Henry was so distracted that by the time she got Rosalie's cage sorted out and got her back into it, she was too tired and it was too late to put on her butterfly costume, though her mother did save all the leftover candy for her.

The next time Rosalie broke out, it was November.

Henry had a play date up at Livy's after school. By the time she started for home, it was really windy and rainy. Henry's mom was working late and Livy's nanny offered to cook dinner for Henry, but Henry knew Rosalie would be waiting at home to be fed, and her dad would never remember. Since she couldn't leave Livy, the nanny gave Henry an umbrella and told her to run, run, run. Holding her book bag while her umbrella turned inside out in the wind, Henry struggled down the driveway with the muddy rain all over the legs of her jeans, and then pulled open the door. She didn't notice Rosalie, out of her cage again, following her inside.

Next thing anyone knew, there were two sets of very wet and muddy footprints leading upstairs—one boot-shaped and one shaped like a lovely fan. "Oh no!" cried Henry.

She thought she'd just rinse off her own legs and Rosalie's, then go to work on the carpet. But by the time she got out of the shower and wrapped herself in a towel, Henry's mom was standing outside the bathroom door with her hands on her hips.

"Well, Missy," Henry's mother said, "I brought home a new video from the library. But *you'll* be washing the carpet until bedtime!"

Through the wall that night, Henry could hear her mother grumbling, and her father saying, "Now, Nancy . . . well, Nancy," the way he did when her mother grumbled. She knew it was her and Rosalie's fault.

She knew that her mom was telling her dad *all* about the muddy footprints and making them sound as if they were the size of a grizzly bear's. She knew how her mom could exaggerate when she was upset, and sorry as she was for upsetting her mother, she was more worried about Rosalie.

Rosalie, my Rosalie, she thought, *please be good. I'll fix that latch. I'll do anything. Just don't get yourself in any more trouble!*

Danger from Above

With help from her father and Livy, Henry used strong screws and a screwdriver to put a new lock on Rosalie's cage, and for a while, things were quiet. January passed, and Henry's father took Henry and Rosalie to the arbor center twice so Rosalie could splash in the icy water with the wild ducks. (She seemed to have a very good time.) As the days got longer, though, Rosalie seemed to get duck spring fever. She even snapped at Henry one day when Henry brought her lettuce! But Henry knew the problem wasn't that Rosalie didn't love her.

The problem was that Rosalie wasn't happy with the big trough of water in her wire run. She wanted to go slipping and swimming in the mud and reeds in the arbor center pond. Sometimes she honked and squawked late into the night, and then Dad started grumbling at night and yawning in the morning. He had to get up early to tend his new plants and make sure the apple trees were warm and safe.

Very early one morning in March, almost a year to the day since Rosalie had come to live with Henry, Henry woke to a terrible screeching and squawking. She ran to her window, which looked down over Rosalie's run, just over the top of the garage.

There, right on top of Rosalie's run, was the biggest hawk Henry had ever seen. And he was digging at the wire mesh with his long claws, while Rosalie ran flapping from one end of her run to the other, in her panic too frightened to run inside.

Henry thought fast. Grabbing the

slingshot her father had made her from a sturdy piece of oak, she slipped one of her little marbles into the band, steadied her arm on the windowsill, and aimed right at that hawk's tail.

Ping! The marble didn't hit the hawk, but it struck so close, he lost one of his long golden tail feathers, and he took off into the dawn sky like a giant spirit, with a whoosh of great wings. Henry ran downstairs, took Rosalie out of her pen, and held her in a warm towel. Rosalie laid her head against Henry's arm, and Henry felt Rosalie's heart slow down until she wasn't shaking anymore. Henry had never been so frightened in her life. "Oh Rosalie, my Rosalie. I won't let anything hurt you. You're only a duck, but you're my piece of luck, and you mean everything to me."

She trudged back to her room and fell asleep on the floor with Rosalie, wrapped in her blanket, until her father came to wake her a few hours later.

He patted Henry's shoulder. "Well," he said, very slowly, "I saw that fracas with the hawk. I'm going to drive you to school. Mom's already gone. We decided to let you sleep in after you were up so early doing battle."

"And?" Henry asked.

"And I'm very proud of you for defending Rosalie. You had a cool wit and a keen eye. But I also don't want my only girl fighting off predators at dawn."

"Dad, why didn't Rosalie just run inside to her cage?" Henry asked.

"I think her instincts were telling her that she was safest if she could get free," said Dad. "See, in her run, Rosalie was basically a sitting duck. The hawk could move all over and attack her, but Rosalie couldn't get away. She couldn't fly or dive underwater."

"But what if she were out in the

wild?" Henry asked.

"She would have gone swimming under a bridge, or dived under the water," her father explained. "Ducks have their own way of solving their problems."

"But she might not have got away," Henry said.

"No, she might not have," Dad admitted, rubbing his chin.

"Maybe I should nail up the flap and keep her inside all night," Henry suggested.

"Well, I think for now that would be a good idea," her father said.

For now, Henry thought. That sounded a lot like the times her mother said, "We'll see."

And so they nailed up the rubber flap. But Rosalie was miserable at not being able to go out for fresh air at night when she wanted to. She pecked and pecked at the rubber flap until it was a rubber rag, and squawked all night at every jogger or car she heard.

One afternoon, when her mother got up from taking a nap on the sofa after school, she said, "Henry, we have to talk."

That never meant anything good.

Henry sat down next to her mother, and they turned off the television show about elephants that

Henry had been watching. "I guess what I'm going to say is going to be very sad. But I have to tell you the truth. I don't think being stuck in the garage and in her run is a very happy life for Rosalie. And we can't drive her to the arbor center for very long, because, in a few months, things are going to get pretty busy around here."

"Dad takes care of the garden," Henry said quickly, "and I take care of Rosalie. I don't see why anything should be any busier than before." She was starting to feel that chilly feeling in her stomach she got in the doctor's waiting room, even though she wasn't really afraid of getting her flu shot.

"It's going to get busier because in a month or so, you're going to have a baby brother or sister," Mom said, all at once.

"I am?" Henry asked, her eyes wide.

"Yes," said Henry's mom, and she pulled off her big blue sweater and Henry saw her slender mom's normally flat tummy was rounded like a little hill.

Henry gasped. Unlike her huge father, her mother was very small. She didn't look like most pregnant ladies. But come to think of it, Henry hadn't been paying much attention to her mom lately, and Mom, who normally was always running around, *had* been exceptionally lazy, and her loose skirts *had* been a little tighter.

"In fact, if you come here, you can feel Mister or Miss You-Know-Who kicking and pushing. Any day now, that little person is going to push right out. You're going to be a big

sister, and I'm going to need your help with caring for our baby. You're big enough to help now."

"Well, is it a boy or a girl?" Henry asked.

"Do you really want to know?" Mom asked. "Wouldn't you rather be surprised?"

Well, I wouldn't have asked if I'd wanted to be surprised, Henry thought. But she said, "I'd like to know. Please."

"It's a little boy," Mom said. "At least that's what the doctor said."

"Well, for heaven's sake, don't name him Nancy," Henry said, more angrily than she meant to. Here she was, getting the little brother she'd wanted her whole life, and she didn't feel happy at all. "So what's all this got to do with Rosalie?"

"Your father and I have been talking, and we think that Rosalie, now that she's grown up, might want to live somewhere that she can spend time with other ducks, like the arbor center," Mom said.

Oh, flop, Henry thought.

But she had to admit, "She does like it there."

"I think she *does* like it there, and though I know you love her very much, we can't let her out anymore. I don't think she likes it here anymore, now that we can't let her out. Do you see, even though it makes you unhappy?"

Henry put her hands over her ears, but Mom gently pulled them down. "I know how much you love Rosalie," she said, looking straight into Henry's eyes. "Loving somebody means doing the best thing for her. The best thing for you, we finally figured out, was to not be the only kid in this house. And I think maybe the best thing for Rosalie is to give her the chance to be with other ducks, the way you'll be with your little brother." Henry's mother pulled her close, even though Henry was too tall to sit very easily on her mother's suddenly not-so-very-big lap. "Letting go of someone you love, even if it's best for her, is the hardest thing in the world," she said.

Henry couldn't say a word. She was crying so hard, her mouth and nose were filled with tears; so her mother just rocked her back and forth, back and forth, very slowly. "Now," said Mom, "let's make a plan."

Rosalie, Living Free

One night in April, Henry's mom said that tonight was the night they would put their plan into action. "If we don't," she said, pointing at her bigger tummy, "we are going to run out of time."

They had already discussed their strategy.

People couldn't just stroll right

into the arbor center during the day and release a duck, especially a white, domestic duck like Rosalie. She stuck out like a sore thumb among the mallards!

So Mom set the clock, and she and Henry got up well before the sun. After wrapping Rosalie in her towel, Mom and Henry drove in the dark to the arbor center. All the ducks were huddled on the bank, sitting with their heads tucked under their wings. Henry set

Rosalie down. At first, she just looked around, and laid her long neck against Henry's knee, the way she had when she was a tiny duckling.

Henry tried to be brave. "Go on, Rosalie. It's okay, sweetie duck. Go on and swim." Rosalie looked up at Henry, smiling her beaky smile. "It's okay. The other ducks will be your friends." Henry opened the bag of grain she'd brought and softly dumped it along the edges of the pond.

That got the other ducks' attention. They came waddling over, one by one, to gobble the corn with Rosalie. "Henry," Mom said, "it's best to go while she's busy and happy."

Henry nodded. "Oh Rosalie, my . . . ," she began, but she couldn't say another word. She took her mother's hand, and they quietly crept back through the gate, and got into the car. As they pulled away, Henry could see Rosalie, like a smudge of lemony-white cloud in the darkish dawn, among all the other ducks, standing a little taller than all of them, like a princess among her subjects.

Henry was in a bad mood all that week. Even learning that she would get the bigger bedroom where Grandma and Grandpa usually stayed—and be able to decorate it any way she wanted—didn't do much to help. Nothing did.

She wasn't hungry.

She didn't want to read the newest books her mother brought home from the library.

She watched TV so much, her mother had to turn off the television.

She took so many showers that she used up all the hot water.

She was too sad to ask to see Rosalie. She was afraid that Rosalie might not remember her, or might have flown away, or worse.

Finally, after what seemed like forever, Henry's mom guessed what was wrong. "You're worried about Rosalie," she said. "You think she might not be okay."

"*Duh!*" Henry said. "She's my own duck, and she's imprinted on *me*, and we haven't been apart since she was practically an egg!"

Mom sat down and put her feet up on the stool. "I think to be fair to Rosalie, we ought to give her just a couple more days to fit in and get used to her new home without bothering her. We don't want to confuse her."

"But what if a hawk has her by now?" Henry asked, throwing down the book she hadn't really been reading.

"Then we can't help her anyhow. And wild ducks know how to band together and seek shelter from hawks and other predators. Little ducklings are in the most danger. And you know, Henry, Rosalie is large for a duck. And she's very strong," said her mom. "I promise if you wait just one more day, we'll go on Sunday to make sure she's just fine."

Saturday passed slowly for Henry.

Livy was in Cancun with her mother, and even the giant postcard Henry got from her that morning didn't cheer her up.

She wanted to go up the hill and tell Dave and Denny that *she* was soon going to have a baby brother of her own. But their baby, Derry, had turned out to be such a brat! She was always swallowing the rubber wheels off the twins' Kar Klassics, and then she would laugh at them when they had to put clothespins on their noses to search for rubber wheels in her diapers. Henry wasn't all that excited about having a sibling anymore.

She wandered up to the golf course on Saturday night and ran into the boy whose toe Rosalie had bitten. He was raking the sand in the sand traps and he stopped to say hello.

"Where's your pal?" he asked, and walked with his toes pointed out for a few steps, like a duck.

"We set her free." Henry sighed. "It was the only kind thing to do. She is at the pond at the arbor center, and—"

"Ouch!" said the boy. "You must feel pretty lousy. I was thinking something like that might happen after my *huge and serious* toe injury." Henry could tell he was making fun of it. "I'm sorry my mom got so upset about a little scratch. She's really a nice person. In fact, I wanted to tell you something if I ran into you again. Well, it doesn't matter now."

"Tell me anyway," Henry said.

"It's just that the reason I work

here is my mom sells all these trees and bushes to the golf course. She has a tree nursery, up past the gray house. She just put a pond in. There are lilies and little frogs, but she's going to get little ducklings, too. Well, I know you must miss your duck," he went on. "You could see the ducklings when they come."

Henry shook her head sadly. "I'm going to see Rosalie tomorrow," she said. "At least that's good."

The boy nodded, then smiled and waved as he got back to his raking.

Next morning, Henry was up and dressed, and had her teeth brushed and her hair combed, by the time the sun came up. When her mother came downstairs, she said, "Somebody's ready to go visit a friend. I have some hard bread here in the bag for the wild ducks, and a little corn for one special one."

As they approached the arbor center, Henry almost climbed out of her seat belt with eagerness. She couldn't wait to see Rosalie, but she wondered if Rosalie had become a wild duck—the princess of ducks— and wouldn't even remember her former human "mother."

As she helped her mom open the old gate, Henry scanned the pond.

There were the green ducks and

the brown ducks and the black ducks. But there was no white duck. Henry looked under the bridge, down among the rushes where the ducks had their nests, and far up on the bank, where they hid among the low river willows. But she found nothing, except a single white tail feather, which could have come from any duck at all.

And then, suddenly, she spotted a thin, gray shadow leaning against a tree. Rosalie's beautiful wings were red with cuts and dark peck marks. Her eyes were closed.

"She's dead!" cried Henry, kicking her way through a knot of the wild

ducks, which scattered wildly. "They've killed her!"

"Wait, Henry!" her mother called. "Wait now. . . ."

But Henry was already on her knees beside Rosalie, her gorgeous, lemony-yellow darling, the only pet she'd ever had.

"The wild ducks must have rejected her," Henry's mom said.

"Mom!" Henry cried, trying to feel for Rosalie's heartbeat. "Just worry about the dumb old baby and go back in the car! I don't want to be mean, but don't explain this to me! I don't care why right now, Mom!" Tears raining from her eyes, she whispered,

"Oh Rosalie, my Rosalie. You may be a duck, but you're my piece of luck, and you mean everything to me. Please, please don't die. . . ."

Rosalie's eyes opened, only halfway, and fluttered, and her sagging beak seemed to lift slightly in its duckly smile. She staggered forward a step and rubbed her long neck against Henry's leg. "Mom, help me! She's alive!"

Henry's mom, who'd stayed to help despite Henry's anger, scooped the dirty, wounded duck up in her skirt, and they ran (Henry's mom sort of waddled) for the car. They drove to the vet's as fast as the signs allowed.

As it turned out, Rosalie was starving. The vet had to put fluid into her body to make her strong again, and feed her mush every day from a dropper until her chipped beak healed. Henry's mother drove her to visit Rosalie every afternoon. Each day she was a little stronger. "She gave them a good fight," the vet told Henry.

Finally Henry and her father came to pick Rosalie up for good. They climbed into the garden truck, Henry with Rosalie on her lap, and drove awhile in silence. Then Henry said, "She's not going back there. Not unless you build me a house in the arbor center and I can live there, too."

"I wasn't going to suggest that,

Henry," her father said slowly. "After all, I was the one who saved her life the first time. There has to be a better solution."

So Rosalie came home.

But she was still a duck.

And she still chased the mailman if Henry let her out.

And she still nipped Scout on the tail.

But she still flopped on the grass.

And so Henry knew she had to think of a plan. But this time, since she was nine going on ten, it was going to be her plan, and it was going to be a good one.

Rosalie in Bloom

The very night Rosalie came home from the hospital, Henry took a long piece of ribbon from her mother's sewing box and fastened it around Rosalie's neck, like a leash. "Yes," she said, "I know you hate it. But you're going to have to be a good girl. If you do, you'll get to go swimming!"

As if she understood, Rosalie, who

still wasn't *quite* herself, padded quietly along behind Henry, up the hill, past Livy's house, and out onto the golf course. The last pair of golfers were just coming in from their game.

"That girl's walking a duck!" one of them called to the other.

"I think you got too much sun, Ed," said his friend.

Henry kept walking until she got to the water hazard near the seventeenth hole, which Rosalie seemed to recognize. Henry then sat with her back against a tree, while Rosalie happily flapped and swam and did duck underwater somersaults in the pond. When it was almost too dark to see, along came the boy in a golf cart. Henry stood up and waved.

"Hi!" said the boy.

"Hi!" said Henry.

"So how is your duck? What's she doing home?" the boy asked. "My name is Will, by the way."

"Well, my name is Henry," said Henry, and when Will opened his mouth, she said, "Don't even bother to say anything about it. About my name, that is. It's a long story. As for Rosalie, it was terrible," said Henry. "The wild ducks at the arbor center practically killed her."

Her swim finished, Rosalie came waddling up out of the water hazard.

She smiled good-naturedly at Will
and then rubbed her neck against
Henry's leg.

"Wow. I see what you mean. She's so skinny! She doesn't look like herself. I'm sorry. She's really a nice duck," said Will.

"She really is, and the thing is, I have to find a home for her where she's *not* going to be pecked at by wild ducks, and she's *not* going to be eaten by hawks, and she's *not* going to be attacked by wild dogs."

"But she can take care of herself," said Will, pointing at his toe.

"Only under the proper conditions," said Henry, who was learning about the environment in school. "She wasn't raised to defend herself in the wild. We all need a little help, you know?"

"Well, here's what I can do, if you want," said Will. "I'll talk to my mom and see if she thinks a big, grown-up duck would fit in with the little baby ducks she got this week. Would you like that?"

"I can tell you right now that Rosalie would fit in. The very thing those little ducks want right now is a great big lady duck to show them the ropes," Henry said with great certainty. Her plan was working!

Will said, "I thought that stuff just came naturally to ducks."

But Henry answered, "No, everyone has to learn. And ducks particularly. Ever heard of imprinting?" Will hadn't, so Henry told him all about it. And he was pretty impressed that she knew so much about science.

The very next morning, Henry and her mother took Rosalie to meet Will and *his* mother, Clare. They lived in a pretty little house behind a tree nursery with a sign in front that read BOUNTIFUL EARTH. There were shrubs and flowering trees of all sizes and shapes, and piles of sparkling rocks and miniature waterfalls for gardens. There were rosebushes in wooden tubs, and a very secure pen, almost like a little house. In the pen were eight darling little ducklings. "I keep them in there at night," said

Clare, "because of—"

"Dogs and hawks and foxes, we know," Henry said. She knew she was interrupting, but she figured it was especially important to share what she knew.

"Why, yes," said Clare. "You sure know a lot about ducks!"

"Well, I learned from this duck here," Henry said, "who is just about the best duck on earth. I mean, she's a great watchduck, so no one could ever rob you." Henry glanced at Will's toe. "She's very kind to people, once she gets to know them, and she's very kind to other ducks, except for mean, savage ducks, like the ones in the arbor center, who tried to kill her when she lived there for only one week!"

"My gosh," Clare said, gently reaching down toward Rosalie's head.

Rosalie, Henry prayed, *don't you dare nip!*

But Rosalie didn't nip. She allowed Clare to stroke her head, and then she waddled away toward the pen, where all the little ducklings were jumping up and down, up and down, waving their stubby yellow wings, just as Rosalie used to do. She looked at the ducklings through the mesh, and then looked back at Henry.

"Do you think I should let them

get acquainted?" Clare asked.

"Well, I guess," Henry said.

Clare opened the pen, and out toddled one little duckling after the other. They all stood around Rosalie, looking up at her. Then Rosalie, as if she were hearing some music only ducks could hear, began marching down to the lily pond. And one by one, all the little ducklings lined up and followed behind her, exactly the same way Rosalie had followed Henry. Smoothly the ducks slid into the water, one by one. When Rosalie kicked her feet, the little ducklings kicked theirs. When Rosalie bobbed her head to catch a tadpole, the little

ducks did the same thing.

Rosalie smiled.

Will smiled.

Clare smiled.

Henry's mom smiled.

And Henry smiled, although it was a smile that was more brave than true. "These are good ducks," Henry said to Rosalie. "They're just like you. They won't hurt you. They

won't peck you. They want to be your friends." And she hoped with her whole heart that this was true. But she couldn't be sure. *Well, Rosalie,* she thought, *at last you're safe. But Rosalie, my Rosalie. You're still my duck, and my dear piece of luck, and you mean everything to me.*

When Mom said it was time to go home, Henry agreed and got into their car pretty quickly and held her head down so that no one could see her face. Will said to her through the window, "Can you ride your bike all the way up here?"

"Uh, since I was *six*," said Henry.

"Well, then you can see Rosalie anytime you want. Did you ever think of that? I know how you feel about her."

Henry suddenly felt a lot better.

She felt the tears melt back down into her throat and smiled at Will. "Thanks," she said. "I'm sure glad that Rosalie bit your toe."

And Will said, "I am, too."

And so Henry would ride her bike up to check on Rosalie every weekend.

Though she was busy with all the ducklings, Rosalie always ran squawking to Henry whenever Henry visited, and laid her long, soft neck against Henry's leg.

When Henry's baby brother was born, Henry's parents let her choose his name. She chose Ross Lee.

"Interesting name," said Henry's father.

"Sounds Gaelic," said her mother.

As soon as Ross was big enough, Henry would ride her bike and Henry's mother would push Ross in his stroller all the way up the hill to

Bountiful Earth, where Clare always had iced tea waiting for them.

While the mothers talked, Henry pushed Ross in his stroller to the edge of the pond. And there was Rosalie, happily bossing around the eight little ducks, which weren't so little anymore, but who still acted as though Rosalie was their queen.

The first time she saw Ross, Rosalie looked a little bit alarmed. And since she'd grown to love her little brother so much, Henry was a little alarmed, too. She picked Ross up and held him close, and gave Rosalie a warning look.

But since she'd spent so much

time at the nursery, seeing new people every day, Rosalie simply walked up and laid her long neck against Ross's chubby leg.

Ross laughed.

Henry laughed.

And then Rosalie smiled up at Henry, as if to say, *Oh Henry, my Henry. You're sweet as can be. You may be a girl, but the best in the world. And you mean everything to me.*